UNICORNS
OF THE
SECRET STABLE
The Great Unicorn Race

JOLLY
FiSH
PRESS
Mendota Heights, Minnesota

By Whitney Sanderson

Illustrated by Jomike Tejido

Book design by Sarah Taplin
Illustrations by Jomike Tejido
Illustrations on pages 17, 29, 32, 52 by North Star Editions

Published in the United States by Jolly Fish Press, an imprint of North Star Editions, Inc.

First Edition
First Printing, 2020

This is a work of fiction. Names, characters, places, and incidents are either the product of the author's imagination or are used fictitiously, and any resemblance to actual persons living or dead, business establishments, events, or locales is entirely coincidental.

Library of Congress Cataloging-in-Publication Data (pending)
978-1-63163-513-7 (paperback)
978-1-63163-512-0 (hardcover)

Jolly Fish Press
North Star Editions, Inc.
2297 Waters Drive
Mendota Heights, MN 55120
www.jollyfishpress.com

Printed in the United States of America

TABLE OF CONTENTS

Welcome to Summerville
Home of Magic Moon Stable

Unicorn Guardians

A long time ago, unicorns and people lived together. When people started hunting the unicorns, two girls decided to help. They used unicorn magic to create a powerful spell. It closed off the Enchanted Realm from the rest of the world. Only the girls' keys could open the Magic Gate.

When the girls grew up, they gave the keys to their daughters. Since then, two young girls have always been the Unicorn Guardians.

CHAPTER 1

Rivals

Ruby led Tempest into a gallop. It felt like they were flying across the meadow. She had Tempest slow down as they went down a hill. Then, they made a sharp turn around a grove of golden-apple trees.

Suddenly, Ruby's sister Iris appeared in front of them. Iris was riding Lyric.

The unicorn was prancing in slow, graceful circles. Iris didn't notice that Tempest was headed right for them.

"Watch out!" Ruby yelled.

Iris looked up. Ruby leaned hard to the left. Iris pulled Lyric to the right. The unicorns just missed running into each other. Iris and Ruby lost their balance and tumbled to the ground.

Tempest and Lyric stopped a short distance away. Ruby got to her feet.

So did Iris. Neither of them was hurt. But their clothes were covered in grass stains.

"You're the one who needs to watch out," Iris said. "There is more to unicorn riding than racing around."

"How would you know?" Ruby asked, brushing grass from her clothing. "You're too afraid to ride fast."

"I am not!" Iris said. She put her hands on her hips.

Just then, a shadow fell over them. Ruby looked up and saw a dragon with rusty-red scales flying overhead. It landed in the meadow next to Ruby and Iris. Tempest and Lyric shied away. The unicorns did not like dragons.

A rider climbed down from the dragon's back. It was their friend Cole. He was the Dragon Guardian.

"Hi," Cole said. "How are you?"

Ruby and Iris glared at each other.

"Fine," they said at the same time.

"You don't look fine," Cole said. He looked from Ruby to Iris. "What's the matter?"

14

"Nothing," Ruby said. "Except that Iris thinks she's the best unicorn rider, but she is not."

"Nothing," Iris said. "Except that Ruby rides wildly and cares more about speed than skill."

Most of the time, Ruby and Iris got along. But right now, they were rivals. Ruby wanted to prove that she was better.

"Maybe you should have a contest," Cole said, "to see who really is the best."

Ruby's eyes lit up. "That's a great idea!"

Iris looked doubtful. "What kind of contest?"

Cole looked toward the mountains.

He thought for a minute. His dragon, Flame Dancer, lowered her huge head to the ground. Her hot breath left scorch marks in the grass.

"I've got it," Cole said, snapping his fingers. "I was just flying over the Diamond Desert. It's on the other side of the Fire Mountains. On the far side of the desert, there is an oasis. It has trees, grass, a lake—and a magical gem. Whoever can reach the gem first is definitely the best unicorn rider."

CHAPTER 2

The Lotus Gem

The next day, Cole met Ruby and Iris in the Enchanted Realm. He showed them a map he had made of the Diamond Desert. He had drawn a big X at the left edge of the map. That was where the race would begin.

To the north of the desert were the Geode Caves. "You can get lost in the caves if you're not careful," Cole said.

At the center of the desert were the Quicksand Pits. "It would be easy to get stuck in the quicksand," Cole said.

Cole had drawn a dashed line below the pits near the bottom of the map. "The safest way is to go around the quicksand," he told Ruby and Iris.

At the right edge of the map was the Lotus Oasis. Cole had drawn a shining jewel in the center of a large pink flower. The jewel was labeled the Lotus Gem. A wavy blue oval surrounded the flower.

"Is that a lake?" Iris asked. She pointed at the blue oval.

Cole nodded.

"It's a good thing unicorns can swim," Ruby said. She was starting to feel a tiny bit nervous. But she would never admit it to Iris.

"We need to choose the unicorns we will ride," Iris said.

"I choose Tempest," Ruby said. "He's so big and strong. He will leave any other unicorn in the dust."

"I will ride Lyric," Iris said. "She's the smartest unicorn I know. She can think fast and avoid trouble."

Ruby and Iris found their unicorns in the herd. They rode together through the Fairy Forest and over the Fire Mountains. Neither of them spoke. They were both thinking about the race to come.

Cole flew ahead of them on Flame Dancer. He landed on the far side of the mountain. Ruby reached Cole first.

She brought Tempest to a halt. She gasped at the sight of the desert in front of her.

The sand was made from tiny chips of diamond. It glittered so brightly that Ruby had to shade her eyes. In the distance was a green smudge.

That must be the oasis, Ruby thought. It looked so far away.

Iris and Lyric walked up and stopped beside Ruby and Tempest.

"I'll wait here," Cole said. "Whoever brings back the Lotus Gem wins the race."

Tempest pawed the ground. Lyric stood quietly beside him. Ruby looked over at her sister. Iris's face was calm.

But Iris also looked determined. Ruby knew that her sister would not be easy to beat.

Cole waited until he saw both Ruby and Iris were ready. Then he yelled, "On your marks . . . get set . . . go!"

CHAPTER 3

The Diamond Desert

Tempest and Lyric took off at a gallop.
Right away, Tempest pulled ahead. His
hooves skimmed the glittering sand.
Ruby's heart raced at the speed. She felt
like even the wind could not catch them.

Ruby glanced back over her shoulder. Iris and Lyric were far behind. Ruby grinned to herself. She and Tempest were going to win!

Tempest came to a sudden stop. Ruby fell forward against his neck. She looked down at the ground. Tempest's legs were buried in wet sand. They had gotten stuck in the Quicksand Pits!

Iris and Lyric galloped past. Iris had remembered to take the longer path around the quicksand.

Luckily, Tempest had stopped at the very edge of the pit. If he had gone any farther, they would have been stuck.

Ruby asked Tempest to back up. It was hard for him to pull his legs out of the sucking quicksand. But one step at a time, he backed out of the pit.

They started racing again. But Ruby's mistake had cost so much time!

Tempest began to make up the lost ground. A smudge of green in front of them got bigger. It was the oasis!

Ruby saw that Iris and Lyric were just ahead of them.

"Come on, Tempest!" Ruby cried. "We can do it!"

With a burst of speed, Tempest swept past Iris and Lyric. Ruby cheered.

Ruby and Tempest reached the oasis. The grass was lush and green. The trees had colorful gems growing on them.

Tempest's strides slowed. He stopped at the shore of a sapphire-blue lake.

A huge pink lotus flower rested in the water. It was just like in Cole's drawing.

Tempest did not hesitate. He plunged into the water and started swimming toward the flower.

Now, Ruby could see the Lotus Gem. It was even bigger than she had imagined. The gem shone with all the colors of the rainbow.

Tempest swam closer to the flower. Ruby grabbed one of the lotus petals. She pulled herself up onto the flower. It was smooth and slippery under her feet.

Tempest let out a nervous whinny. Ruby felt like he was trying to warn her about something. But she was so close. The Lotus Gem was right in front of her. She could win the race and beat Iris.

With a shout of triumph, Ruby reached

out and grabbed the gem.

As soon as she touched the gem, the earth rumbled and shook. The sky darkened. A strong wind began to blow.

Ruby stared down at the gem in her hands. It had turned the color of storm clouds.

She knew that she had made a terrible mistake.

CHAPTER 4

Sandstorm!

Ruby put the Lotus Gem back where she had found it. But the rumbling and shaking did not stop. The wind swirled even faster.

Ruby ran to the edge of the flower.

She jumped onto Tempest's back, and

he began swimming toward the shore.

The water had been calm, but now tall

waves crashed against them.

When they reached the edge of the lake, Tempest did not stop to shake himself off. He began to race back across the desert.

Stinging sand hit Ruby's back. The wind sounded like the roar of wild animals. Ruby huddled close against Tempest's back.

Where were Iris and Lyric? Ruby could not see them. She could barely see anything. The sand blew into deep drifts under Tempest's hooves.

Ruby was afraid. Even Tempest was not fast enough to outrun this storm.

Just then, a shape appeared beside her. It was Iris and Lyric.

"Iris!" Ruby cried. But the loud wind made it impossible for Iris to hear her.

Lyric's shoulder bumped against Tempest's. Lyric was making Tempest turn to the side. Now, the sand stung Ruby's face instead of her back. Lyric was telling them they had been going the wrong way.

Tempest stumbled and almost fell.

The sandy path was getting too deep for him to run. Soon, the storm would swallow them up.

Ruby spotted something shimmering ahead. It was the entrance to a cave! The inside was filled with purple crystals.

Tempest and Lyric struggled through the sand. At last, they reached the safety of the Geode Caves. Outside, the wind kept howling. But the storm could not harm them here.

Ruby saw tunnels leading into the cave.

But she stayed near the entrance. She remembered Cole's warning about getting lost.

Finally, the storm stopped. Ruby and Iris rode out of the cave. The desert was still and calm again.

"Look!" Iris said. She pointed to the sky. A red shape was flying high above them.

Ruby and Iris shouted and waved their arms. Cole saw them. Flame Dancer flew down and landed in a deep drift of sand.

"I'm really sorry," Cole said. His eyes were wide with fear. "The Lotus Gem must be under a spell of protection. When the storm started, I flew over the desert to find you. But I couldn't see anything through the sand."

"It's okay," Ruby said. "Thanks to Iris, we found shelter in the Geode Caves."

"It was Lyric," Iris said, patting Lyric's neck. "I was trying to outrun the storm.

But Lyric remembered the caves. She guided us to safety."

"Maybe you're the best rider after all," Ruby said. "You listened to what your unicorn was telling you."

Iris shook her head. "You reached the Lotus Gem first," she said. "If it wasn't for the sandstorm, you would have won the race."

"Either way, I'm glad you're both okay," Cole said.

"Should we head home?" Iris asked.

Ruby nodded.

After saying goodbye, Cole and Flame Dancer took off again.

Ruby and Iris rode side by side through the desert. They reached the Fire Mountains and headed toward home. Iris ran a hand through her ponytail. "My hair is full of sand," she said.

"Mine too," Ruby said. "Tempest and Lyric are also covered in sand. We should swim in the pond when we get back to the meadow."

Iris grinned. "There's no reason we can't finish our race," she said. "Last one to the meadow is a rotten egg!"

Iris urged Lyric into a trot along the rocky path. Laughing, Ruby followed on Tempest. This time, she was careful to watch where she was going.

The race was on!

THINK ABOUT IT

 Ruby is good at riding fast. Iris is good at riding smart. Which skill do you think is more important?

 Write about three skills that you are good at. Then write about three skills you respect in other people.

 Tell a friend about a time you were in a contest or race. It could have been in school, in sports, or at home.

ABOUT THE AUTHOR

Whitney Sanderson grew up riding horses as a member of a 4-H club and competing in local jumping and dressage shows. She has written several books in the Horse Diaries chapter book series. She is also the author of *Horse Rescue: Treasure*, based on her time volunteering at an equine rescue farm. She lives in Massachusetts.

ABOUT THE ILLUSTRATOR

Jomike Tejido is an author and illustrator of the picture book *There Was an Old Woman Who Lived in a Book*. He also illustrated the Pet Charms and My Magical Friends leveled reader series. He has fond memories of horseback riding as a kid and has always loved drawing magical creatures. Jomike lives in Manila with his wife, two daughters, and a chow chow named Oso.

RETURN TO
MAGIC MOON STABLE

Book 1

Book 2

Book 3

Book 4

Book 5

Book 6

Book 7

Book 8

AVAILABLE NOW